DIPPED IN HOLLY

DANA ISALY

CONTENT WARNING

This book is only for those over the age of legal adulthood due to its graphic sexual content. There are themes such as bondage, age gap, Daddy kink, and, as always, a lot of bad words. All characters are well over the age of eighteen.

"I WANT MY CHEEKS CLAPPED, DADDY. (CLAP 'EM)"
-PPCOCAINE

CHAPTER ONE

HOLLY

UNTHINKABLE BY CLOUDY JANE

DANA ISALY

I look at myself in the mirror and start to list off everything I don't like about myself, each a perfectly acceptable reason for Josh to have left me tonight, five days before Christmas, at his friend's Christmas party. I don't even have any of my own friends out there. He's left me alone in this fucking bar.

"You have a crooked nose," I tell myself in the mirror as my mascara continues to pour over my cheeks. "He definitely didn't like your rolls and stretch marks. He would always make fun of your freckles and the scars your acne left behind. Are you really that surprised?" My dirty-blonde hair hangs in waves over my shoulders, and my normally grey-looking eyes are a brighter blue from crying. At least they look pretty.

Swings and roundabouts.

I choke back a sob. Five fucking years of my life wasted with someone who was fucking his secretary for two of them. My sob turns into a laugh. Oh my God, do all of his friends know? Are they all out there right now talking about how pathetic I am to have not noticed?

A knock comes from the door, making me nearly jump out of my skin.

"A minute!" I shout at the locked door, my voice coming out a bit wild even to my own ears. Jesus, Holly, chill the fuck out. To be fair, I'd be pissed, too. I am in a communal bathroom, and I've hijacked the entire thing for myself. I wipe away the streaks of mascara from my cheeks and roll my eyes at my ruined makeup.

That, combined with the outfit I'm wearing, really makes a great impression. I can't wait to make my way home by myself dressed as a slutty Mrs. Claus, complete with thigh-highs, a miniskirt, and a corset top that is about to break my ribs after all the sobbing I've just done.

Another couple of knocks, louder this time.

"Can't a girl get five minutes to have a mental breakdown in peace?" I yell as I stomp toward the door and swing it open, coming face-to-face with a man. My eyes travel down his body and back up until I meet his eyes again. It's like he's chiseled from fucking stone.

His hair is salt-and-pepper, along with his short beard that outlines his sharp jawline. He's wearing black jeans and boots, with a flannel button-up. The sleeves are rolled up, exposing his tanned and very muscular forearms. His hazel eyes watch me take him in for a moment before he speaks.

"Few customers complained the bathroom door was locked," he says, looking behind me like he's going to find someone else in here with me. My entire body flushes as I realize he probably thought I was fucking someone in here.

"Who are you? The boss of the bathrooms?" I ask him, pushing past him and into the hallway, trying to hide my quickly reddening cheeks.

"Well, I'm the owner of the bar, so I guess I'm technically the boss of the bathrooms, yeah," he says, his chuckle a deep rumbling sound that makes my stomach flip.

Fuck, I think to myself. Of course he's the owner.

"I'm sorry," I tell him, turning around to face him now that I'm under the cover of the dim lighting in the hallway. It's at the back of the bar, filtering out the majority of the music and conversation from the front. "Girl stuff," I say, cringing at how that came out.

He crosses his arms, and his head tilts as he looks me up and down, making me suddenly feel extremely aware of just how slutty my slutty Mrs. Claus costume really is. His lips form a smirk that is pure sex.

"Okay," I drawl. "I'm gonna take off." I take a step backward, and he follows the movement with his eyes. I turn around, but suddenly, his hand is around my arm—his extremely warm, calloused, strong hand. It's wrapped around my bicep, and as I turn around to look at him, he drops it like I burned him.

"Stay."

It's not a request; it's a command.

"Why?"

"Because I want you to," he says like it's the most obvious thing in the world that he would want me to stay.

"No, thank you," I say, taking another step back. "Those people out there aren't my friends, and I was just dumped, brutally so, right in front of them. So, I think I'll just head out."

"No," he says, grabbing my arm again, sending heat through my body. "You won't. Have a drink with me at the bar. Show them you're not so easily defeated."

Five minutes ago, I was bawling into a bathroom sink over an asshole, and now a whole other type of cocky asshole is standing in front of me, bossing me around, and my pussy is already aching for him. His voice and the confident way he holds himself make me consider saying yes. What the fuck is wrong with me?

"That's settled, then," he says, moving his hand from my arm to my lower back as he leads me back out to the main area of the bar with a gentle shove in the right direction.

"I don't remember saying yes."

He laughs, and the vibration from it travels through my body, lighting me up like a Christmas tree. I'm thankful he's behind me because I know what I'm like when I'm under the attention of someone I deem far out of my league. I can feel how hot my cheeks and chest are, and for him to see me respond like that to him would mortify me.

Get yourself under control, Holly.

I'll blame it on not having great sex in years. Really, I haven't even had good sex. Josh and I started off sort of strong in that

4

department, but after a year, I couldn't be bothered anymore. I've been worried I have low sex drive, but maybe that isn't the case if how I'm responding to this complete stranger is any inclination.

"I promise I don't bite unless you ask me to," he says, his mouth suddenly very close to my ear. So close, in fact, I felt his hot breath flutter across my skin. I flinch, the sensation startling me. He chuckles. "What's your name, Red?"

"Holly," I tell him, pretty proud of myself for managing to say it without my voice breaking.

"Festive," he answers. "I'm Nick. Here, come over here." He directs me through the crowd and to the very end of the bar, where he pulls out a stool for me. Making his way around the bar, he looks at me and winks.

"What do you drink, Holly?" he asks. I try not to look around to see if Josh and his friends are still here, but I can't help myself. I look out of the corner of my eye, trying to make it look like I'm just getting comfortable, but all-knowing-Nick calls me out.

"They're in the corner," he says, leaning across the bar and grabbing me by the chin. This time there's no escaping it—he sees my skin turn a horrifying shade of pink under his gaze. "You wear your emotions on your sleeve, don't you, Red?" he asks, brushing the back of his finger across my cheek before leaning back.

"How do you even know who they are?" I ask him.

"You think I didn't notice you the second you walked into my bar?"

5

I swallow, and his eyes follow the movement.

"What'll it be?" he asks, his smile showing off a dimple in each cheek that I didn't notice before. Was this man chiseled from the dreams of a thousand women or what?

"Rum and Coke," I tell him, pushing my hands under my legs to stop myself from fidgeting. "Dark rum, please. Spiced, if you have it."

"What kind of bar would I be running if I didn't?" he asks before turning his back on me to make my drink. I try to resist, but I can't. I glance over to the corner and find them all laughing and joking, cozy in their little corner bubble.

Josh must feel my eyes on him because it isn't but ten seconds and he turns, locking eyes with me from across the bar. A sick feeling forms in my gut all over again, making tears threaten my vision. His gaze is empty and uncaring, and that cuts me all over again.

But then there's a mouth on my cheek, warm and a bit scratchy from a beard. I swing my head toward it, and Nick catches my mouth in a kiss before I can protest or ask him what the actual fuck he thinks he's doing. Not that it matters because his lips are soft and, God, I want him to keep going. I don't care that he's a stranger and that I met him while I was crying over my ex because this kiss is everything. This is the kiss. This is the kiss that makes you realize you've been missing out your entire life on having the shit kissed out of you.

His mouth opens, and our eyes meet. It's the most erotic thing

I think I've ever done, kissing a stranger while my ex watches, with my eyes open. His hazel eyes are on mine, and his pupils are blown, sending a bolt of lust down my spine. His tongue swipes over mine, and I let him, relishing in the way he tastes like whiskey and the slightest hint of peppermint. He takes my bottom lip between his teeth gently, and I stifle a moan.

"There," he says, pulling away abruptly, leaving me to fall forward in my chair. He winks again and slides my drink in front of me. "Now the last memory he has of you will be watching you melt for someone else."

DANA ISALY

CHAPTER TWO

DANA ISALY

NICK

FREAK SHOW BY ALEXANDER LEMA

DANA ISALY

She looks at me with shy but hooded eyes that turn my already hard dick to stone. I heard her through the bathroom door, saying mean shit about herself while she cried, and while I told myself it was just a fatherly instinct kicking in, that was clearly not true. I didn't want to kiss my kids the way I had just kissed Holly. The way I want to kiss her again, and again.

Christ, she's definitely young enough to be my kid. She has to be at least half my own age if I'm guessing correctly. Her eyes move from me to her drink as she picks it up and downs the entire thing in one go. I barely put any liquor in it, not wanting her to sit here and get drunk over the asshole in the corner.

I don't let myself think it's because I want her sober for what I want to do to her once I get to kick everyone out of here in an hour. It's definitely not because I'm considering asking her to stay...with me.

Fuck.

I watched the way the kid had handled the situation, first denying anything, and then I saw his body language change as he admitted it. Everything happened in front of his entire friend group, and if the way they responded was anything to go off, they had very clearly known or at least suspected.

"So, Nick," she says, pushing the glass back toward me and gesturing that she'd like another. She seems to have recovered from the embarrassment for the time being. I start thinking about other ways I can get that reaction. "Do you always do this? Is this, like, your thing?"

"Is what my thing?" I ask, refilling her drink. I chuckle at her, unable to help myself when her inner brat comes out to play.

"You know," she says, gesturing toward my body. "The whole sexy stranger, come with me and I'll kiss you silly thing." She's impersonating my voice, and I just stare at her and smile.

God, the things I want to do to her.

"You think I'm sexy?" She blushes and narrows her eyes on me. "Not normally," I tell her, moving on and putting her out of her misery. "But I thought I'd make an exception for Mrs. Claus, seeing as it's Christmas."

"Spirit of giving."

"Exactly." I lean my arms on the bar and watch the way her throat bobs as she swallows the drink I put in front of her.

My eyes trail down her body, loving the way her skin flushes every time she catches me staring. Her breasts are pushed up and together, thanks to the stiff corset top she's wearing, and with each deep breath, it's like they're begging to spill out. I want to reach across the bar and set them free, palming them and tweaking the perfect nipples I know she's hiding under there.

When was the last time I had a one-night stand? I'm far too old for that shit now, but I let my imagination wander to spending the night with her. An image of her sweet face looking up at me while she kneels at my feet flashes in my mind. My cock throbs painfully against the zipper of my jeans.

"You're staring," she says, bringing my eyes back up to her face that is burning red.

"Am I?"

"You are. See something you like?" she asks, her voice dripping with sarcasm.

"I see a lot of things I like," I tell her, enjoying the way her eyes widen in surprise. I lean in closer to her, watching her pupils dilate and her breathing pick up. I hope the kid in the corner is watching. I wonder if he was able to make her feel like this. Is she wet? What I wouldn't fucking give to taste her.

"How about some water?" I ask her, my eyes gesturing to her drink. There may not be a lot of alcohol in there, but it's hard to turn off my dominant instincts in a situation like this.

Her hand trembles as she lifts the glass back to her lips and finishes it off before answering me.

"Okay."

When I hand her the glass of water, I catch movement in the corner of my eye. I look up and spot him walking over toward us.

Without even thinking, I'm around the bar and between him and her before he can reach her.

"What...?" I hear her ask as she realizes what's happening. "Oh, fuck off, Josh," she says, trying to push me out of the way. Funny that she thinks she can. I'm an ex-Marine, and there's no way in Hell either of them is getting past me. But the way her hands warm my skin through my flannel is distracting. I give her a look over my shoulder, and she rolls her eyes, going back to nursing her water.

"Who the fuck are you?" Josh asks me, trying to get in my face but falling half a foot too short.

"Not someone you want to fuck with, kid. Leave the young lady alone." I hear Holly snort behind me.

"I'd listen to him, Joshua!" she sings over my shoulder. "He's the owner of the bar, and he'll kick you and your lying, cheating ass out!"

Okay, she's a lightweight.

"Drink your water," I say over my shoulder.

"Don't tell her what to do, man."

I turn my attention back to Josh and cock my head. This kid seriously has a death wish because my anger is a hard beast to control once it comes out to play. And it wants to play with him. I take a step toward him, close enough for our bodies to touch if either of us breathes too deeply. I feel her small hand wrap itself around my bicep, and his eyes find it.

"Go home, kid," I tell him, smirking down at him. "We're

closing soon anyway. Leave her alone. I'll make sure she gets home." I didn't think about it before I said it, but it's true. I will make sure she gets home safely. I may just have some fun with her first.

"I knew you were a fucking mistake," he spits at her, and I feel her recoil like the words bit her. "Fucking slut," he murmurs as he walks away.

I crack my neck and shake off her hand.

"Yeah, that's not gonna fly with me," I say aloud before grabbing his arm, spinning him around, and tossing him over my shoulder.

People around us start laughing as I push past people to the front door. His friends are on their feet when they see us walk past. My bouncer, Seth, opens the door, shaking his head like this isn't the first time he's seen me do this. Which, I guess is true. I have a short fuse, and instead of fighting, I've learned to just throw them out of their ass. It tends to leave a more lasting impression.

I let him drop to the cold concrete and ignore his insults. His friends can take care of him from here.

"He doesn't come back in," I tell Seth. "Ever." He nods, and I pat him on the back as I walk past him. Holly is still at the bar, staring at me with wide eyes and her mouth opening and closing like a fish. I notice her water is gone.

Good girl, Holly.

"You deserve better," I tell her as I pass right by her and go

back behind the bar. I give her another glass of water. "Drink."
I turn and start viciously cleaning everything in sight. I need to
calm down before I throw her over my knee in front of everyone
and redden her ass for dating someone so pathetic.

The thought only sends me spiraling again, thinking about her
spread open for me as I land smack after smack on her soft skin,
my handprints covering her ass. I bet her whimpers would turn
into moans as I kneaded her sore flesh and slipped a finger inside
of her...

I drop a glass, the shards flying everywhere, and sigh as I hear
her laugh behind me.

CHAPTER THREE

HOLLY

YOUR GUILTY PLEASURE
BY HENRY VERUS

DANA ISALY

■ Favorite color?" I ask him.

"Blue."

"Of course it is," I snort. "Every man's favorite color is blue."

"Yours?" he asks me. I can hear the smile in his voice from across the bar. He's closing everything down. The bar closed about thirty minutes ago, and he sent everyone home. He asked me if I wanted to stay.

I said yes.

"Green. But not the bright lime green. Like a forest green, or a sage green." I sit up from the booth I'm lying in and watch the way his back moves as he wipes down the shelves behind the bar.

I pull my eyes away, looking around at the decor of the place without people cluttering up the place. It's bathed in deep reds and warm wood. It has a speakeasy-type feel with glowing Edison bulbs and heavy velvet curtains blocking the view to the street outside.

"How old are you?"

He turns around and looks at me, raising an eyebrow and leaning back against the counter.

"I just turned fifty," he says, narrowing his eyes on me and smirking, waiting for my reaction.

I shrug and stand up, walking over toward him.

"Wizened," I say with a smile, teasing him.

"Hah!" he barks out, throwing the rag into a bin. "Old," he says, watching me slowly walk the length of the bar, running my fingertips on the glossy wood.

"Vintage." My smile grows as I look at him. Whatever dance we're doing, I like it. I like the way my heart beats faster under his gaze and my skin heats with a delicious warmth that spreads into other places, places I would most definitely like to feel the soft scratch of his beard.

"Ancient," he counters as I round the corner and enter into his space. He's gone still, watching me with his eyes but keeping his arms over his chest and his legs crossed at the ankles.

"Established," I murmur as I get within touching distance of him. His eyes lick up and down my body, and I swear I can feel them as if his hands were on me. I want them on me. We've been playing this game of tug-of-war for the past half hour, and I'm ready to let go and have him pull me in.

"Experienced." His voice has taken on a whole new tone, and it causes the butterflies in my stomach to go crazy. He moves slowly as I approach him, turning so that my back is against the

24

counter and his arms are caging me in. The clean scent of his aftershave invades my senses and makes my head dizzy.

"Oh, yeah?" I ask him, my voice only wavering a little. "How experienced are we talking here, old man?" My voice is teasing, but his eyes aren't. They're trained on me like he's the hunter and I'm his prey. "Could you change my tire? Check my oil?"

"Baby girl," he murmurs, his voice rumbling through my body as he presses a hand to my stomach, letting it trail lower as he speaks. I can't look away from his eyes no matter how nervous I am. He has a hold over me as he pushes his body even closer. "I could take apart everything under your hood and put it back together better than I found it."

His hand dips under the band of my skirt, and his fingers dance over the soft lace of my panties. I'm embarrassed at how wet I am and have been ever since I saw him in the hallway. He runs his fingertips over the fabric covering my slit before teasing the sides.

"Holly," he says, leaning forward and brushing his lips over my cheek. I sigh and drop my head back, hoping he'll move his mouth to my neck. "If I dip my fingers inside of these lacey panties, am I going to find you wet for me?"

He presses openmouthed kisses down my throat while running his fingers up and down the sides of my underwear. It's the lightest touch I think I've ever experienced, and the teasing is about to send me over the edge. I'm wound so tight I think I could come just from the anticipation and his mouth on my neck.

Pulling back, he uses his free hand to gather my hair at the base of my neck. He grips it taut and makes my eyes meet his.

"I asked you a question."

"Yes," I breathe, needing his mouth back on my fevered skin. He leans in, so close to kissing me that I can feel his breath skirt across my lips. I try to lean forward and close the gap, but his fist keeps such a firm grip that I can't. I whimper and pout, wanting him to give in.

"Don't be a brat, Holly," he says, the smirk on his lips making those dimples pop again. His fingers in between my legs just barely make their way onto my bare skin. "Yes, what?"

Deciding to test the waters, I smirk right back at him, and instead of trying to move my head, I just stick out my tongue. I lick the seam of his mouth and then my own, humming and biting my bottom lip.

"Yes, Daddy."

"Fuck," he moans before he's on me like he needs me to breathe. His fingers finally slip underneath the lace and find me soaking. "Holly," he growls into my mouth, swirling my wetness up and around my clit, making my knees weak. "You're so wet, sweet girl."

He's everywhere, in between my thighs, at my mouth, against my body, and in my lungs. His tongue pushes inside my mouth for the second time tonight, and I surrender to him, letting him fuck my mouth the way I want him to fuck me on this counter. A finger slides easily inside of me, and I break the kiss to moan loudly at how good it feels.

He pulls his finger free of me and offers it to my open mouth. I greedily suck it between my lips, tasting myself on his skin while I tease him with my tongue, letting him know just how much I wish it were his dick instead. His eyes watch my mouth, his hazel irises almost completely eclipsed by his pupils, giving him a dark look that sends a new rush of aching heat between my thighs. I'm fucking throbbing for him, and my nipples are tight and pebbled, seeking his attention.

He picks me up, spinning and sitting me down on the main bar before he settles his hips between my legs and kisses me again. His fingers work the ties of the corset, working it looser and looser until I can finally take a deep breath. He gets frustrated and begins to pull it apart, ripping the fabric and finally pulling it loose enough that it can be yanked over my head. I laugh at his eagerness, but he just takes a moment to look me over.

"God, you're perfect," he whispers, running his knuckles over the pointed tips of my nipples and then across the red lines the bones of the corset have left on my skin. I gasp at the sensation and let my head roll back as he replaces his fingers with his mouth. It's hot and wet as he sucks my breast into his mouth, swirling his tongue around the peak before taking it between his teeth.

I roll my hips into his, desperate for some friction. I can feel that he's hard, and the sheer size of him is almost worrying. He takes the other nipple in his mouth, and my hands find his hair. Running my fingers through the soft strands, I tug and pull as I try to get closer to him. With each pass of his tongue over the tip, my pussy clenches, making me a needy, whimpering puddle.

His mouth is on mine again, his lips warm and wet from the attention to my breasts. He spins me around so that my back is facing the long length of the bar and helps me lie down. He situates himself between my legs again and slowly begins to pull off my thigh-highs, kissing down my leg until he gets to the ankle, and begins the process all over again on my other leg.

"I'm going to show you exactly how a man should treat a woman," he says as he pulls my panties off. He tosses them aside, and I'm left in nothing but my miniskirt, my legs wide open for him as my heels sit on the bar.

"Look at that perfect cunt," he groans, his head dipping between my thighs and inhaling my scent. I blush furiously from the tips of my toes all the way to the top of my head as I feel his nose run the length of me. He takes my hands and places them in his hair.

"I want you to fuck my face," he tells me as his lips brush the most sensitive part of me. "You will tell me what you like, you will squeeze my head with your thighs, and you will tug on my hair so hard that you're worried you'll pull it out."

He pauses.

"And Holly?" he asks, looking up at me over my skirt, his eyes so full of lust it makes my pussy clench.

"Yeah?" I breathe.

"You will scream for your Daddy when you come. Understood?"

DANA ISALY

CHAPTER FOUR

NICK

I WANT TO
BY ROSENFELD

DANA ISALY

Her pussy is fucking perfect, pink and glistening with her arousal, and she has the softest blonde curls that I run my nose through. I lick straight up her center before sucking her clit into my mouth. She cries out, squeezing my head with her thighs and arching her back off the bar.

She grinds her hips against my face, lifting her head up off the counter to watch as I eat her out like a starving man. We make eye contact as I slip a single finger inside of her, curling it until I feel the soft pad of her G-spot.

"Do that while you make circles around my clit," she tells me.

"Like this?" I ask her, using the tip of my tongue to do exactly as she asked while my finger teases that spot inside of her.

"Yes, thank you, Daddy," she moans. My cock feels like it's going to rip right through my jeans. It's so stiff and ready to sink inside of her. I can feel how tight she is by the way she clenches around my finger, and I can't wait to watch her stretch for my cock.

I push another finger inside of her, slowly scissoring and stretching her as I listen to the sweet sounds of her moans and whimpers. I alternate between circling around her clit and sucking it, getting her closer and closer to the edge each time. There's a sheen of sweat across her body and a flush creeping its way across her chest and up her throat.

"You're close," I growl, and she nods, throwing one of her arms over her face. She takes that plump bottom lip between her teeth and bites it as she groans deep in her chest.

I keep up my rhythm, eager to see what she looks like in the throes of her orgasm. Her breath picks up, her chest heaving with the effort as her belly moves with her hips. She bites on her hand before I move my free hand up, shoving my fingers into the wet heat of her mouth.

"Use me," I beg her, and she does. She sucks and bites on my fingers with vigor, matching the rhythm I'm using on her pussy. I pull them out of her mouth, wiping the spit across her mouth before shoving them back in. "Good girl," I praise.

"Oh, fuck!" she moans around my hand as I feel her pussy flutter around my fingers. "Yes, Daddy!" she cries out as I nibble on her sensitive and swollen clit. My dick leaks into my boxers as her taste explodes across my tongue.

"You taste so fucking good, baby girl," I tell her as the last of her orgasm pulses through her body. She bites down hard on my fingers, and I groan against her soft flesh. I pull my fingers free of her cunt and lick them clean before lifting her boneless body to a sitting position.

I take my fingers out of her mouth and kiss her, letting her know just how sweet she tastes. Her tongue swipes over mine before sucking it into her mouth a few times. My dick takes notice of her tease, twitching painfully against my denim.

"I want to taste you," she murmurs against my lips, her hand finding the length of me and stroking it. I push into her hand, and a growl escapes my throat. I drop my forehead to her shoulder as she continues to move her warm hand up and down.

"Upstairs," I say, pulling her off the bar. She wraps her legs around my waist and kisses me as I blindly try to find my way to the stairs that lead to my apartment above the bar.

"I feel like now is a bad time to ask you if you're a serial killer," she says, a little laugh coming from that sweet mouth.

"Definitely should've asked that earlier," I tell her. "Too late now." I pull the keys out of my back pocket and open the door that leads upstairs. I shut it behind us and carry her up the dim stairwell.

"Do you live above your bar?" she asks as we make it to the landing, and it opens up into my living room.

"I do."

I kick off my boots, and then I'm shutting her up with another kiss. I carry her to my bedroom and let her stand on the floor next to the bed. She watches me as I unbutton my shirt and let it fall to the floor.

"Take off my jeans," I tell her.

Her cheeks redden, but she takes a step forward and places a hand on my chest, running her fingers through the grey hair there.

"I like your tattoos," she says as she traces over the now faded lines and colors of all the ink I got while on tour.

She takes her lip between her teeth again as her hand dips lower, making my abs jump at the light touch. She breathes a soft laugh before unbuttoning my jeans and pushing them off my hips. My boxers are tight and do nothing to hide just how excited I am to have her here with me.

Getting to her knees, she hooks her fingers under the band of my boxers and slowly pulls them off. Her eyes go wide as my erection springs free, hitting the tip of her nose. I step out of everything and kick my clothes to the side as I grab the base of my cock.

Holly looks up at me with those big grey eyes, and I run the tip of my dick across her open mouth, smearing my precum on her lips. She maintains eye contact, waiting for me to tell her what to do next.

"Taste me."

Her hand comes up to replace my own, and I thread my fingers through the soft strands of her hair, silently guiding her where I want her. The tip of her tongue runs up my slit, collecting what has leaked there into her mouth. She moans as she swallows it down before wrapping those soft lips around my head and sucking me to the back of her throat. She gags a little but continues on, humming and moaning around my cock, the vibrations going straight to my spine.

Her mouth feels like heaven as she takes me in and out, swirling the flat of her tongue around the sensitive underside of my tip before sucking me back in. I put one foot on the bed behind her, giving myself better leverage to move in and out of her throat. Her free hand is planted on my hip, and I guide it between my thighs, showing her how I want her to play with my balls.

"Fuck, baby girl," I moan the second she catches on and takes over.

She licks me from base to tip, my cock wet from her spit, and then strokes me as she adjusts and begins to lick and suck on my balls. The leg holding me up nearly buckles at the sensation.

"Okay, you need to stop," I tell her, knowing I'm going to come if she keeps it up. But she doesn't stop—she doubles her efforts, speeding up her hand and sucking harder with her mouth. "Holly," I growl, pulling tightly on her hair.

I'm too weak to stop her as I feel the beginning of my orgasm wash through me. Feeling my balls tighten in her mouth, she lets go and swallows my dick into the back of her throat. She gags and coughs, spit drooling out of the corners of her mouth. The tightening of her throat is my downfall; it pushes me over the edge, and I spill into her.

I push forward, fucking into her as deep as I can as she

swallows everything I give her. When I pull free of her, cum and drool strings from her lips to my dick, and the sight makes my cock twitch. She eagerly leans forward and cleans me up. "Was that good for you, Daddy?" she asks me, her face a perfect mask of innocence. She knows what she did, and her teasing makes my dick want to go for round two. I always did have a thing for taming brats.

"It was, baby girl," I tell her as I wrap my hand around her jaw, pulling her up off the floor. She leans into me and licks her lips. "But you didn't listen when I told you to stop."

"You didn't actually want me to stop," she says, a smirk playing on her mouth.

Brat.

I lean down and kiss that smirk off her lips, tasting the saltiness of myself on her tongue. Her hands go to my waist, her fingertips digging into my skin as she begs me to come closer.

"Doesn't matter," I tell her, pulling away and looking into her confused gaze. "When I tell you to do something, I expect you to listen." She swallows. "Now I have to punish you."

CHAPTER FIVE

HOLLY

PUT IT ON ME BY MATT MAESON

DANA ISALY

44

My breath picks up at the promise behind his words. I've never been with anyone like this before—dominant and confident—and it's something I've always been curious about. Even though I'm nervous about what type of punishment he's talking about, I can't help but be extremely curious.

He kisses me again while his hands explore my body, running down my back and squeezing my ass. He is so solid and warm against me, I feel far safer than I have with anyone in my past. Which I do realize is slightly crazy seeing as he's a complete stranger, but there's something in the way he carries himself, and the way he treats me, that makes me feel like I can be myself with him.

"Stay here," he says, breaking the kiss and giving one of my nipples a playful pinch before he leaves me standing next to his bed.

I look around his room, taking in the surprisingly stylish

decor. It's warm and feels like a home instead of the bachelor pad I thought he would have. The walls are painted black, and he has a wooden headboard and a perfectly made bed with plenty of pillows. I wonder if they smell like him, and I'm tempted to lie down and curl up.

But I can hear him making noise outside in the living room area, so I stay perfectly still until I hear his footsteps approaching again. When he comes into view, he's holding a long string of Christmas lights, smirking as he watches me try to figure out what his plan is. I'm not sure how this is going to work into my punishment.

"You're cute when you're confused," he says, finally making his way over to me. I roll my eyes at him, and he just lets out one of those deep chuckles that make my knees weak.

"Are you going to make me decorate your apartment as punishment?" I ask him.

"As much as I would like to see you walking around my place naked doing domestic things, I had something else in mind, baby girl. Lie down on the bed, facedown."

I do as he says, making sure to make a show of crawling onto his bed with my ass swaying in the air. He breathes out, and I hear a little groan escape him before I settle into position.

"Arms behind your back," he commands.

I do as he says and turn my head to watch him as he plugs the multicolored lights into the outlet next to the bed. He stretches them out, and the bed dips under his weight as he climbs behind me.

He grabs a couple of pillows and lifts my hips, placing them underneath me so that he has a better view or better access—either one I'm okay with as long as he touches me soon. I'm starting to crave his warm and calloused hands on my skin.

He begins to tie me up with the lights, looping and twisting them around my arms until he reaches my wrists. The rest of the lights continue on over and under my hips before they go down my right leg and he ties them off.

Nick kneels behind me, groping and squeezing my ass, using his thumbs to spread me apart for him. That little stretch makes my pussy pulse with need. He blows cool air across my heated flesh, and I shove my face into the covers and moan. When I inhale, I breathe in his scent, and it turns me on even more.

I've never done anything like this in my life. I've never had a one-night stand or let anyone, especially a stranger, tie me up in bed. I've never called anyone Daddy, and I definitely haven't ever orgasmed as hard as I did downstairs on his bar. It's reckless, and yet everything about him turns me into a puddle at his feet.

"I'm going to spank you five times," he tells me, and I can feel my body tremble. I've had fantasies like this—what girl hasn't? But being faced with it in the moment? It sends a terrifying mixture of excitement and need through my entire body.

"Okay, Daddy," I breathe. Fuck, why do I like calling him that so much?

"I want you to count for me, okay, baby girl?"

His hands lightly skim over the flesh he's about to redden with his palms. I wonder if I'll be sore tomorrow? Will he spank me hard enough to mark me? To cover my ass in his handprints? I fold my fingers together and take a deep breath.

"Yes, Daddy."

"Good girl."

I hear the smack before I feel it. It makes me jump, and the sting is immediate and hot until his hand kneads and massages the area. My nipples tighten with the sharp tingle of pain, and I can feel myself get even wetter.

"I told you to count, Holly." His voice is deep and full of warning.

"One."

He spanks me again, this time harder but in the same exact spot as last time, and I whimper and try to move forward out of instinct to get away from the pain. He massages the spot again, and I moan into the sheets.

"Two."

The third slap surprises me as it lands on my opposite cheek. I let out a shocked yelp before I feel his lips on my heated skin, his tongue outlining what I imagine is the handprint it left behind.

"Three," I whisper.

My stomach is tight with need, and my pussy is clenching and aching for him. I expect another slap, but instead, one of his fingers teases me, circling my soaked entrance before slipping inside of me. I sigh and push back on him, waiting for him to move, but he just holds it there inside of me, driving me crazy with frustration. I groan and push back only to be met with the hardest slap yet.

"Four!" I cry out, clenching around his finger and pushing my face into the mattress until I can barely breathe.

Fuck, fuck, fuck. My ass is on fire.

He kneads and massages the cheek he slapped, all the while keeping his finger sheathed inside of me, completely still, just fucking teasing me. I can feel myself getting wetter with each slap, and my desire to feel him move inside of me is all-encompassing. I can't see past my own need for his dick.

The hardest slap comes last, nearly sending me through the fucking headboard.

"Five!"

"Such a good girl," he praises me, and I can't help but roll my hips, trying to get off on his teasing. "I can feel your pretty little pussy gripping onto my finger like the needy little thing you are. I like you like this, Holly," he says, slipping his finger free of me. "Whimpering and desperate for me."

I feel him shift on the bed, and his mouth is on me, biting and licking over the entire reddened area he left in his wake. He slowly makes his way across my ass before dipping lower, his tongue circling around my asshole before pushing into it. I gasp at the new sensation. No one has ever been back there...ever.

I'm suddenly very self-conscious, and I try to pull away, but he grabs my hips and pulls me back to him, shoving his face even deeper before coming up for air.

"You don't get to deny me what I want to eat. I'm hungry. Let your Daddy feast on you." He groans and continues his sloppy assault, licking, biting, and sucking every inch of me.

His tongue dips lower, lapping up my juices as he teases my aching cunt. When the tip of his tongue glances across my clit, I moan and push back into his face. I need him to stop teasing and get me off already.

"Please, Daddy," I beg him, my words muffled by the blankets.

"Please what?" he asks before sucking my clit between his teeth. The pressure in my core builds to a painful heat. His hands massage and grip my thighs as he continues to lightly suck on my clit.

"I need to come, please." My voice is strained, and I feel on the verge of tears.

"Not yet," he says, suddenly pulling away from me.

I lose all coherent thought, crying out into the bed below me and trying to grab him in awkward angles with my legs. He laughs at my outburst and falls forward as I catch him off guard. His dick, hot and heavy and so fucking hard, presses into the crack of my ass, and I push back on it, grinding and hoping it'll find its way further down.

"Temper tantrums won't get you anywhere, little girl," he says, humor filling his voice as he regains his balance and pulls away. "I want you to be so wound up that you're brainless with lust, ready to do anything for my cock to be inside of you."

"Please," I whine, but instead of giving in, I feel the bed shift and move as he climbs off it.

He comes into my view, bending down to my level, and smiles. He's so fucking handsome it hurts. Leaning in, he kisses the tip of my nose and pushes my wild hair out of my face, tucking it behind my ear.

"You were such a good girl for me, Holly," he says in a calming voice that brings me back into myself bit by bit. "You took your punishment so prettily, and seeing your ass marked up with my handprints?" He moans and runs his fingertips over the lights wrapped around my body.

"Please, touch me," I beg him, closing my eyes as the lights tickle my skin.

"Oh, I will, baby girl," he assures me, his hand coming back so that he can run his thumb over my cheek. "But, first, I'm going to take my time with you."

CHAPTER SIX

NICK

CHILLS – DARK VERSION BY MICKEY VALEN, JOEY MYRON

I roll her over on her back, keeping her tied up in the lights. I like the way they light up her skin in a soft glow. I reposition the pillow so that her hips are still elevated. They'll give my mouth easier access and give my dick a better angle for when I finally let myself sink inside of her.

She looks up at me with hooded eyes, waiting to see what I'm going to do next. I can smell her sex in the air as I push her thighs apart. I lick my lips, still able to taste her there as I run my hands down her legs and across her hips, moving them onto the soft curve of her stomach.

Goose bumps break out across her skin as her breathing picks up. She arches her back as I get closer to her breasts, trying to push them into my hands. Her nipples are pebbled and make my mouth water to be on them. My dick leaks as her hips roll into me and brush her sweet pussy against my aching length.

She's going to be the death of me.

"I'll be right back," I tell her, taking a deep breath and rolling off the bed.

"Where are you going?" she asks, her voice full of nerves.

I lean over her and take her mouth in a soft kiss. She's putting a lot of trust in me as a stranger, letting me tie her up and leave her alone. I know a little bit of fear turns her on, but I don't want her to worry that I'm going to abandon her. I don't want to overtake her desire.

"I'll be right back, I promise. I'm just going downstairs to get something, okay?" I smile down at her, and she bites her lip again. I pull it free from my thumb. "That drives me crazy, you know." I kiss that soft bottom lip. "We're going to keep this little Christmas theme going," I tell her with a smile that I hope calms her nerves.

She smiles back and nods. I hurry downstairs, not wanting to leave her for longer than I need to. I grab the mistletoe from above the front door and then on a whim grab a candy cane from the bowl of them sitting on the counter. That will give her something to suck on while I have my fun.

Holly eyes what I have in my hands as I make my way back into my room. I climb back onto the bed, hovering over her body and holding the mistletoe above her mouth. She smirks and moves her face closer to mine. I open my mouth for her, and she explores with her tongue before taking my lip between her teeth.

"I like the way your beard feels," she whispers before kissing me again. I watch her kiss me and revel in it. When I saw this girl a couple of hours ago, I never thought I'd be lucky enough to have her in my bed. And now here she is, wet and begging for my dick with every move her body makes.

I break the kiss and tear the plastic seal of the candy cane with my teeth, peeling the wrapping off completely before tracing it over her lips. She opens her mouth, and I let it move just inside, watching as her mouth closes around it and she eagerly sucks it inside. My dick twitches as I feel her tongue move around it.

"Now you have something to suck on while I tease you." I smirk when she rolls her eyes, trying to pretend like she isn't as affected as her body tells me she is. "And it'll keep you quiet."

She grunts, and I move the mistletoe down to her throat, letting my mouth follow the movement. I hold it over each part of her body that I want my mouth on. Her collarbones, her nipples, in between her breasts, and across her ribs.

I can hear her breathing heavily through her nose as her mouth remains wrapped around that candy cane. It stains her lips an even darker shade of red. Moving the mistletoe down her belly, I trail hot, openmouthed kisses down to her belly button before taking the soft flesh at her hip into my mouth and biting down.

Her hips arch up, her pussy seeking friction anywhere they can find it as a long groan moves through her body. I chuckle against her skin and continue my way down her body, kissing and licking everywhere except exactly where she wants it. She has cute pink stretch marks that color the inside of her thighs, and my tongue traces them as I shift further down her legs. I kiss under her knees, on top of them where I find a scar on one, and then down her shins to her ankles.

When I stop and look back up at her, her eyes are squeezed shut in concentration, and that candy cane is twirling around between her lips. When she realizes I've stopped, she opens her eyes and looks down at me, taking a bite of the candy and crunching on it with a look of irritation.

"What's wrong, baby girl?" I ask her, trying to hold back my amusement. "Am I not touching you where you want?" I crawl back up her body and pull the half-eaten piece of candy from her lips and taste it.

"You know you aren't," she whines, shuffling her body below mine as she tries to get contact with my skin. I smile down at her and plant soft kisses across her face before I make my way back to her lips. She's eager for it, swallowing me whole as we taste the sweet peppermint on each other's tongues.

"I told you," I say against her mouth as I use the wet, broken tip of the candy to scratch across one of her nipples. "I want to tease you until you can't take it anymore." I blow cool air across her nipple, and she moans at the soft burn of the peppermint.

"I'm at my limit, Nick," she says, looking at me with pleading grey eyes.

I can hear the frustration in the tone of her voice, and it goes straight to my cock. I toss the candy cane and mistletoe to the nightstand and situate myself fully between her thighs.

"Condom?" she asks. "I've been with that asshole for so long I stopped using birth control."

"I had a vasectomy years ago," I tell her as I stop my advances to look in her eyes and get a read on her. I don't want to wear a condom—I want to feel her grip and pull on every inch of me as I push inside of her. But I would never push her to do something she was uncomfortable with. "But I can use a condom. Would you be more comfortable if I used one?"

"Thank God," she moans as she takes my mouth with hers. "No." She looks into my eyes, and I can see the determination in them. "I want to feel you as you fuck me for the first time."

"For the first time?" I ask her, my voice playful as I grab the base of my dick and push it through her slit and toy with her clit. "So you want this to happen again?" I wag my eyebrows at her, and she laughs. I may be teasing her, but the thought of keeping her to myself for more than a one-night stand has my heart trying to beat its way out of my chest.

"What do you want from me, baby girl?" I ask her before she can say no and ruin my hopes. Her eyes darken, and her legs wrap around my waist, the lights digging into my skin like fingernails. I tease her, letting just the tip of my cock push inside of her before pulling out and running it over her clit.

"I want you to fuck me," she says, her eyes glossing over with need. "I want you to sink into me, stretch me, and fuck me until I forget my own name. I need you to make me forget." Her eyes plead with me.

I let the tip sink into her once more before pulling it back out.

She groans, and I smile at the annoyed look she's giving me. It's just as hard for me to deny her because with each little thrust I give her, my entire spine lights up with pleasure, sending waves of heat through my groin and abs. But hearing her beg is worth it.

"Beg me for it," I tell her.

"Daddy, please," she whines, her voice cracking on the last word. "Please, I need it. I need you, please. I am empty and aching for you. I need your cock to fill me and stretch me. Make it hurt. Make me yours."

With that, I lose all sense of control. I slam into her in one swift thrust, forcing my way inside of her. I'm big, much bigger than she was ready for, and she cries out of the intrusion, her pussy clenching around me until I think I might lose it and come on the spot.

"Oh, fuck!" she growls through her teeth, her hips rolling up and her head falling back. Her mouth opens, and I take the opportunity to grab it with my own. I kiss her deeply as I pause inside of her, letting her get accustomed to my girth. Her chest heaves against my own, our sweat mingling as we both try to get control of our bodies.

"Sweet girl," I moan as I kiss down her throat. "This pussy," I say, letting my fingers move between us and tweak her clit. "This pussy is mine now."

"Yes, Daddy," she moans as she begins to move her hips in little rotations. It's such a tight fit inside of her that every little movement threatens to send me over the edge. I take a few deep breaths as her cunt pulses around me, pulling me in as deep as I can physically go.

"My God," I murmur against her heated skin before pulling away and sitting back on my heels. I need to feel her fucking hands on me. I quickly unwrap the string of lights from her leg and then lift her hips as I pull her free. She moves her arms, helping me untangle the damn things before we both start laughing.

I pull her up so that she's sitting on my cock instead and use both hands to pull the rest of the lights from her body. She laughs and wraps her arms around my neck and kisses me. I thrust up into her, and she gasps as her hands tug and pull at my hair.

She pulls away from the kiss as I thrust up into her again. Her hands go to either side of my face, and we lock gazes before she speaks.

"Fuck me, Daddy."

CHAPTER SEVEN

HOLLY

DESIRE – SLOWED BY HUCCI

He's so big I feel like I'm being split in half but in the most delicious way. He has filled me like no one else ever has. He's addicting in every way, from the way he smells to the way he tastes. It's like he's my own personal brand of catnip.

Both of his arms wrap around my back, and he lowers me down onto the bed, maintaining eye contact the entire time. He looks at me like he's trying to consume me from the inside out. As we move together, he shifts inside of me, touching a spot I didn't know existed. Pleasure soars through my body, and I gasp as I arch against him.

"I know, baby girl. I know," he murmurs. He moves again as my legs wrap around him and pull him closer, hitting that same spot. My mouth falls open, and I can feel my eyes roll back. He caresses my face and my hair as he leans over me on his elbows and continues to push inside of me deep and slow.

My hands run down his back, my nails digging into his flesh

as I feel his muscles flex underneath them with each movement. His head drops as he nuzzles my neck, nibbling and licking my pulse point as the pleasure builds in my core.

"Nick," I whisper. "Fuck, Nick."

"Yes, Holly," he says, my name sounding like sin coming out of his mouth. He meets my eyes and takes me in before his mouth finds mine again. The way he watches me as he kisses me is so fucking erotic, like he couldn't dream of missing a single moment of whatever this is. Like he wants to see every little reaction I give him.

The slow pace he keeps between my legs is torturous, and every nerve in my body is on fire from it. I raise my hips off of the pillows with each thrust, forcing him as deep as he can go. With each drive inside of me, a spark of both pleasure and pain mixes together, pushing me violently toward the edge of my orgasm.

"I need you to come," he tells me as he grabs my breast, bringing a nipple to his mouth and sucking. I throw my head back at the added sensation and run my hands through his hair.

"Hey," he says, his hand suddenly gripping my jaw and bringing my gaze to his. "These eyes stay on me while I'm inside of you."

He thrusts harder, his hips smacking into mine.

"Every reaction is mine," he says, driving into me harder than before. The pain crashes through me, making my pussy throb around him with pleasure.

"Every noise you make is mine."

Another thrust.

"Every single orgasm I rip from your body," he growls with another push inside of me. His eyes are glued to mine, heated with his pupils blown wide with need. My breathing picks up as the beginning of an orgasm begins to roll through me.

"Every single orgasm is mine." His hand moves from my jaw to my throat, squeezing the sides. "Give it to me," he commands. "Come."

I don't break eye contact as I come, giving him exactly what he wants.

"Just like that," he says, hitting the same spot over and over again as I come. "Look at you. So pretty." His voice is full of awe as he looks at me. His hand moves to my hair, wrapping it in his fist and pulling it taut.

He kisses my mouth, and then his lips are everywhere, my cheeks, my jaw, my throat. His pace picks up as he chases his own pleasure. My hands are all over him, running across his chest and down his back. I move them back to his face as he kisses me again, our tongues invading each other's mouths.

"Are you going to take my come like the good little girl I know you are, Holly?" His voice is a strained growl and makes goose bumps break out across my skin. One of his hands goes between us to tease my clit, circling it with the lightest touch.

"Yes, Daddy," I breathe against his mouth.

Suddenly he switches positions, sitting back on his heels and pulling me with him so that he can watch as our bodies move together. Both of his hands knead my thighs as he continues to pump into me. One of his thumbs finds my clit, making me sigh in relief as tingles begin to spread through my body all over again.

"I want one more from you, Holly," he tells me as his abs ripple and dance with his thrusts. "I know you can give me one more, baby girl. Come with me."

I let my hands reach up and trail down his stomach. He grabs my arms and lifts me forward so that I'm sitting on him. Each time my hips roll, my clit grinds down on him and makes me moan into his mouth.

"You're so fucking beautiful," he tells me in between kisses. "You're perfect."

"Fuck, Daddy," I whimper, feeling his praise sinking into my bones.

"Everything about you," he murmurs against any skin he can find. "Everything is so fucking perfect for me."

"I'm going to come," I tell him, digging my nails into the back of his neck as I ride him and take what I need. His hands move to my hips, helping me move up and down on him. His muscles bulge and flex, and I'm lost. One hand goes to his hair, and I pull it hard, forcing his eyes to mine, just like he did with me.

"Come with me, Daddy," I beg him.

His hazel eyes take me in, and then he attacks my mouth, holding my body close as my orgasm triggers his. I grip and squeeze him, and I feel him spill into me with a groan. His cock twitches inside of me, and my body almost goes limp, boneless and sated from what he gave me.

I've never had sex like this in my life.

"Me either," he says, and I realize I must've said it out loud.

Our foreheads touch, and we stare at each other. I can't tell what he's thinking, but suddenly I feel awkward, like I should climb off him and let him get some sleep. Is that what happens with one-night stands? Does the girl leave?

I blush thinking about all the things we said to each other, all the things we did together, and most of all, how many times I called this man Daddy in the last hour. I can feel myself turning bright red, and he watches it with a smirk.

"Why don't we take a shower?" he asks me, running his hands through my sweaty hair. I really could use a shower. I'm covered in sweat, my makeup is a mess from crying and fucking, and I'll have his cum dripping from between my legs very shortly.

"A shower sounds nice," I tell him, moving to get off him.

"Where do you think you're going?" His arms lock around my body, pulling me back against him.

"To get a shower," I tell him like it's obvious.

"I've got you, baby girl."

Next thing I know, we're off the bed, and I'm still impaled on his dick as he carries us to the adjoining bathroom. I look around as he leans in and starts the water. It matches the bedroom in its white-and-black theme. There's a couple of pairs of jeans and flannels on the floor. He catches me looking, and a soft blush spreads across his cheeks.

If I ever thought he couldn't possibly be more handsome, this blush proves me wrong. I run my thumbs over his cheeks and then poke his dimples.

"You're blushing."

"I wasn't expecting company," he tells me as he tests the water and then finally steps inside. He lets me stand and begins to wet my hair.

"You don't have to wash my hair."

"I take care of what's mine." My stomach does a little flip, and I shut that shit down because I just got dumped, and I'm not about to entertain the idea of catching feelings for the rebound.

"And at least for tonight," he continues. "You're mine."

CHAPTER EIGHT

DANA ISALY

NICK

RENEGADE – SLOWED + REVERB BY AARYAN SHAH

▌▌Keep your hands right there," I tell her as she lazily opens her eyes. I've never slept so soundly with someone lying next to me. She let me hold her all night, and the feel of her soft body against mine was extremely comforting. So when I woke up this morning and saw she was still here, still wrapped in my arms and still sleeping, I decided to wake her up in the best way I knew how.

"Hi," she says, her voice full of sleep.

"Hi," I say as I slip a finger inside of her. Her back arches off the bed, and she moans as her eyes flutter closed.

The hand that was holding her arms above her head moves down as her soft skin breaks out in goose bumps. Her eyes open and watch me as I add another finger, and my other hand plays with her nipples. That dirty-blonde hair of hers is spread out on the pillow in a tangled mess of waves like a halo.

She's beautiful like this, still sleepy and bare-faced, her skin flushed with desire. My thumb begins to play with her clit, and her hips roll against my hand, trying to get me exactly where she wants me. I smile down at her and slip free of her cunt.

I bring my fingers to my mouth, and her taste explodes across my tongue. Her pupils expand, and she licks her lips as she watches me, taking that bottom lip between her teeth.

"I need you," I tell her, crawling down the bed and pushing her legs wide. "Hold your legs here for me, baby girl."

Her hands immediately go behind her knees, holding herself bare and open to me. My thumbs spread her even further apart, exposing the wetness that has already gathered there. I lick her from her ass to her clit, tasting every sweet inch of her before I delve my tongue into her center. She groans and pushes against my face as I fuck her with my tongue.

I will never get sick of the way she tastes or the way her moans have the cutest little breathy quality to them, like she's almost shocked every time one comes out of her mouth. I groan and growl into her as I eat her out, letting the vibrations roll through her.

My dick is hard as a rock, and I can feel it dripping onto the sheets underneath me as I grind my hips against the mattress. Looking up at her, I watch as she plays with her nipples. Her eyes are locked on the way my mouth moves against her.

When my tongue dips back inside of her, she sighs and her head drops back. I wrap my arms around her hips, holding her in place as she gets closer and closer. Her moans fill the room, and her hands find my hair, pulling until I can feel my eyes watering at the sting. It only adds fuel to the fire, my hips curling into the mattress with each swipe of my tongue inside of her.

"Yes, Daddy," she moans, her hips bucking against me with vigor.

The way she calls me Daddy even in the light of day makes my cock throb. Fuck, I want to be her Daddy. I want to taste her like this every morning before I take my time as I sink into her wet heat over and over again until she is screaming and writhing underneath me.

"I'm coming," she struggles to get out as her breathing picks up, her chest heaving and her abs rolling. I don't stop; I continue the same rhythm as I work her through it. She holds me close to her as she comes, my tongue diving inside of her to get as deep as I possibly can.

Her pussy throbs around my tongue, and she gasps as her legs begin to shake around my shoulders. I keep going, pulling every last bit of pleasure out of her that I can. She cries out and tries to get away, pushing on me instead of pulling, and I laugh as I let her go.

"Too much," she says between heaving breaths.

I give her one more lick, pressing the flat of my tongue against her clit, causing her to scream again and wiggle against my grip. I suck it into my mouth, and she playfully slaps me across the back of my head.

When I pull my mouth free of her and we lock eyes, she can see she's made a mistake. The arousal in her eyes begins to mix with fear.

"Did you just slap your Daddy?" I ask her, slowly moving up her body, my beard almost dripping with her cum. I bite the soft skin of her stomach, and she gasps. Kissing the hurt, I move further up and do it again and again until I'm at her neck. I bite down on her sensitive pulse point, pushing my dick against her thigh and claiming her like a caveman.

The thought of her running into her ex with my teeth marks on her skin drives me mad with a possessive lust that has me doing it over and over again, all over her neck until she's writhing beneath me.

"I want anyone that sees you," I tell her, pausing to bite her again. She moans, and my hips move further up to slip and slide against her cunt. "I want them all to see you've been marked and claimed."

"Fuck," she moans, rolling her hips up to meet mine.

"Do you like that, baby girl?" I ask her, doing it again as the head of my dick grazes her clit.

"Yes," she says on a gasp.

"Yes, what?" Our hips roll together again, and the very tip of me slips inside of her.

"Yes, Daddy," she corrects herself, moving her hand between us and gripping my cock. Her soft hand is warm, and when she strokes me, my forehead falls against her shoulder. Pleasure spikes down my spine and right into my balls. I resist the urge to take her in that moment and fuck her into the bed.

Instead, my hand finds hers and pulls it away. I lift my head, and our eyes meet, both hooded with lust and need. It takes all of my self-control to not give in. Instead, I pull back and flip her over, using my arm to lift her ass in the air.

"I think you deserve another spanking for that little outburst, don't you?" I ask her as I run my hands over her ass. She pushes back into me and moans as I spread her wide, taking in my new favorite view before I give her her punishment.

"Yes, Daddy," she says in a pitiful little voice that makes my dick twitch. She's too fucking good at this.

"Count."

The first slap lands...hard. Last night was a test to see how much she could take, and she had taken it like the good little slut I hoped she'd be.

"One," she moans, her back arching even further as I knead my handprint.

I smack her again, hard enough to leave a very visible handprint. She barely gets the word out before I land number three in the exact same spot as the first two. This time she yelps and tries to move away.

"Three," she whimpers.

"We're going to ten," I tell her in a stern voice. "If it gets to be too much, tell me yellow to let me know you're getting close to your limit and red for me to stop immediately."

"Yes, Daddy," she says.

I want her unable to sit comfortably for the rest of the day, so my slaps continue to land in the exact same spot, turning her ass bright red. The skin heats under my palm, and I relish in her whimpers of pain and arousal.

When we get to seven, I give her a short break. But when I look down to see her pussy dripping for me, my blood heats to an unbearable level. I can see it literally dripping from her slit, and it takes everything in me to not bury my face back between her thighs. Instead, I keep going, my hand landing harder on her sore skin.

"Eight!" she screams into the pillow, her voice raw from the pain. But she doesn't use the safe words I gave her, so I go again, landing slap number nine. My handprint is bright red on her, and my cock is heavy and throbbing at the sight.

"Nine!" Her voice is muffled this time, and I look down to find her biting on the pillow beneath her. I know she's almost at her limit—I can tell by the way she flinches each time my hand comes in contact with her ass. The last one is the hardest I've landed, making my own palm sting.

"Ten!" she sighs, her hips pushing back toward me.

My hands gently rub and knead her tender flesh as I watch her wetness continue to drip out of her and down onto the blankets beneath us. There's a small puddle there, and I think it's the sexiest fucking thing I've ever seen.

"You are positively drenched, baby girl," I tell her as she moans at my touches.

"Please," she begs, her hands going out to her sides and fisting the sheet. "Fuck me. I need your cock, please."

My cock strains at the need in her voice. I grab her hips with one hand and my dick with the other, lining us up. I watch her pussy grip my length as I slowly slip inside of her with ease. She's wet and hot and fucking perfect for me. When I'm in her to the hilt, I pause, staring down at us where we are joined.

"Fuck," I moan as her pussy pulses around me.

She takes matters into her own hands and begins to pull herself off me before pushing back. I let go of her hips and watch her move on and off me, fucking me exactly how she wants to. The noises filling the room are wet and sloppy as she picks up speed.

"Pause," I tell her, and she does, stopping with my dick completely sheathed inside of her. "Relax," I say as I spit down onto her ass and move it around with my thumb. I want to see both of her tight holes stretch for me. I need to claim all of her before she leaves.

As I push the tip of my thumb in, her noises become small and pathetic. I continue to work my way in, letting her become accustomed to the burn before pushing in a little bit further.

Once I'm completely inside her tight little hole, I move it inside of her and listen to her groan so loudly that it vibrates through her entire body. Her cunt twitches, and my balls tighten. This isn't going to last much longer if I don't get myself under control.

"Good girl," I praise her as she remains still, but her breathing picks up. "I'm going to fuck you now, okay? And you'll take it so prettily for me, won't you?" I run my free hand up her back.

"Yes, Daddy."

CHAPTER NINE

HOLLY

ALL MINE BY PLAZA

That's all the warning he gives me before he pulls almost completely out and slams back in. From this angle, it makes me see stars. Between that and the full sensation he's giving me with his thumb, I'm already close to coming again.

He fucking me so hard and so fast, I can barely keep up to meet his thrusts. My face is pushed into the pillow, and I grip onto the sheets with my hands to make sure I don't go through the headboard.

I'm so wet that he slips in and out of me with ease, stretching me and filling me like no one else ever has. I turn my head and watch him as he thrusts in and out of me. His eyes are focused on where we're joined as he licks his lips.

There's a soft sheen of sweat on his torso, and I can feel a heat spread through my body as I watch his muscles move and flex. Those faded tattoos and his greying chest hair do something for me.

When he sees me watching, he moves his thumb inside of me and smirks as my breath catches. I feel myself blush as he continues to fuck me in both of my holes. He reaches forward with his free hand and gathers my hair, pulling it back so that my back arches even harder for him.

"I wish you could see how perfectly we fit together."

His praise floods my veins with pleasure, and I know I'm close to coming again.

"Nick," I breathe as I snake a hand back to my clit and begin to play with myself.

He slows his punishing momentum as I chase my release. It builds and builds and builds as he continues to stroke every nerve inside of me, hitting the exact spot I need him to over and over again. I'm mindless with it. I'm absolutely brainless with the need to come.

As it racks through my body, he holds his dick steady inside of me. I feel myself break into a sweat as it pours through me, making me squeeze and flutter around him.

"Good girl. What a beautiful little thing you are, Holly. Your pussy is so perfect when it's gripping me, trying to milk me for all I'm worth."

He continues to murmur praises as it finally subsides and I can breathe normally again. I blink away the stars from my vision, and my body goes lax as he lets go of my hair. I fall against the pillow and take deep, steadying breaths.

He lets me rest just a moment before I feel him slowly pull

himself free of me. His arms wrap around me and flip me over onto my back. Situating himself between my thighs, he runs a hand down my side and then lifts one leg around his waist as he pushes back inside of me.

We watch each other as we both gasp before he kisses me. My hands run up his chest and then into his hair. God, I love his hair. It's cropped shorter on the sides but on top there's enough to grab and pull my fingers through. And the way he moans when I do that sends shock waves through my body.

He breaks the kiss to look at me as he continues his slow torturous thrusts. His hazel eyes look more green in the warm light of the morning, and they hold me captive. I'm overcome by a stupid amount of emotion that I try to swallow down. But he sees it.

"I know," he murmurs before kissing me. "Me, too, baby girl."

Somewhere this morning, our fucking turned into something else. We can both feel it, and I think it scares both of us. But he just continues to kiss me as I lift my hips to get him deeper with each push.

"Come with me," he says in between kisses. His tongue sweeps inside my mouth, and we explore each other. His entire body moves against mine with each stroke. "I need you to come with me, Holly."

His need triggers my own, and when one of his hands moves down and begins to circle my clit just the way I like it, I can feel the orgasm begin to build. Our mouths are open, both of us feeling our need to come together like a perfect storm as our lips barely touch each time he pushes inside of me.

"You're close," he says, and it's true. I'm right on the precipice. I'm teetering on the edge, and he can feel it in the needy way I whimper and move against his fingers that keep teasing me.

He chuckles when I moan in frustration, and the vibration rumbles through me. I love that cocky little laugh he does. I grip his jaw and pull him down for a kiss, my tongue fighting against his in a war. He pinches my clit, and I'm gone.

I cry out into his mouth as my orgasm catches me by surprise and crashes through my body. I can't help but bite down on his lip as his hips stutter and he comes as well, feeling him empty himself into me as a growl comes from his chest. He stops, and his head drops onto my chest as the rest of his body falls on top of me.

We're both breathing heavily, and I laugh as his full dead weight lies on me. I run my hands down his back, feeling the muscles there jump under my touch. His arms wrap around me as he breathes me in and plants little kisses across my chest.

"I'm starving," he finally says, breaking the comfortable silence we had fallen into. "Come to breakfast with me."

I look out the window to my left and see there are flurries falling and think about how I literally only have my slutty Mrs. Claus costume. I snort at the idea of going to breakfast with him in my little miniskirt and corset.

"What's so funny?" he asks, shifting so that he can look at my face. The adjustment makes him move inside of me, and I feel myself jump at how sensitive I am from the past however many hours I've been here.

God, what time is it? How long have I actually been here?

"I only have my slutty costume from last night," I tell him, looking around the room for a clock. "I don't really think that's proper breakfast attire." I blink at the clock on the wall, trying to get my eyes to focus. It's only eight in the morning—no wonder I still feel like I could sleep a few more hours. My body isn't used to this anymore.

"You can wear something warm of mine, and I'll take you home first to get changed. There's a quaint little diner I like to go to that's on the other side of the city." He kisses me.

"Can't fight that logic," I tell him, finding that I don't really want to. I'm not ready for whatever this is to be done yet. I think I'd like to talk to him, get to know him a little bit better as a person without his dick inside of me.

Not that I'm mad about the dick.

"Good," he says, sliding out of me and off the bed. "Hold on, let me get you a towel, and then we can clean up and head to yours."

I lie there and stare at the ceiling as he fetches me a towel from his bathroom. My stomach is doing a hundred different kinds of flips at the idea of spending more time with him. It's like Cirque du Soleil in there.

Even though my body seems to be excited, it's hard to get out of my own mind. It seems ridiculous to be excited about another guy after I was dumped less than twelve hours ago. Not that Josh and I even really had a relationship anymore. We hadn't had sex in probably six months; we didn't even sleep in the same bed anymore because he was always up playing video games until three in the morning and he didn't want to wake me up.

Us going to his Christmas party was the first time we were seen out together since Covid. I can't even remember the last time we ate dinner together or laughed together. We didn't share stories anymore, we didn't watch TV together. God, we could barely stand to be in the same room together.

Looking back, I know I was just holding on to something that I was terrified to let go of because I didn't know where I would end up. Realizing I could've been in the arms of a silver fox? I'm sad it didn't end sooner.

"You should probably stay in the car," I tell him as he begins to clean me up with a towel. I blush, wishing he'd let me do it in the light of day, but when I try to take it from him, he shoos me away.

"You live together?" he asks, tossing the towel into the corner.

"Yeah, we were together for a long time," I say, letting the bitterness seep into my tone.

He nods, staring out of the window like he's deep in thought about something before finally speaking.

"Let's get showered."

CHAPTER TEN

DANA ISALY

NICK

ALL I WANT FOR CHRISTMAS IS YOU BY MARIAH CAREY

She walks out of her house with two massive suitcases, an angry expression on her face, and her hair blowing in her face despite the beanie she's thrown on. I jump out of my car and help her, telling her to get in where it's warm while I put them in the trunk.

Jesus Christ, they're heavy.

"What happened?" I ask her as I climb back into the driver's seat.

"She was there," she tells me as I drive off in the direction of the diner. It's snowing hard now, coming down in huge white flakes. We may finally get a white Christmas. "I decided just to pack as much of my shit as I could stay at my parents' over Christmas, and then I told him I would be back for the rest."

"Good, I'm glad you have your family to rely on." I offer her my hand, and she looks at it a moment before taking it, lacing our fingers together and taking a deep breath. My chest swells with happiness when I feel her squeeze my hand.

"Sorry," she mumbles, looking over at me with sad eyes.

"Why in the world are you sorry?"

"Just...could you possibly take me to my parents' after breakfast? They don't live that far from here."

"Of course, Holly. I'll take you anywhere you want to go." I give her hand a squeeze for reassurance, and she nods, turning her attention back out the car window.

The rest of the ride is silent, both of us watching it snow. I glance over at her a lot, unable to keep my eyes off her. She's dressed in a simple outfit of boots, jeans, and a soft sweater. But I can't get over how beautiful she looks in the soft light.

When we get to the diner, I jog around the car and open her door for her. When she steps out, she stands on her tiptoes and purses her lips, making a kissing noise. I smile and take her face in both of my hands, kissing her softly before throwing my arm around her and escorting her inside.

The diner is warm, and the scent of coffee and pancakes hits us as we walk in.

"Nicky!" Wanda comes walking up to us, eyeing Holly as she takes me in her arms. "Haven't seen you in a while. Who's the pretty girl?"

Holly blushes under the attention.

"This is Holly," I say, smiling down at the soft pink coloring her cheeks. "Holly, this is Wanda. We've become pretty good friends over the years I've been coming here."

"It's so nice to meet you," Holly says.

"It's about time he brings a lady with him," Wanda says as she walks us over to a booth in the corner. "We were all beginning to think he'd be alone in that bar for the rest of his life." She doesn't give me time to talk back before she's saying something about coffee and walking off toward the counter.

"Wow, you come here often, huh?" Holly asks, her face lighting up with humor.

"Probably more than I should," I tell her, handing her a menu.

We make small talk before ordering. Holly gets the

snickerdoodle pancakes, and I get my normal breakfast platter. I watch her as she stares out of the window and sips on her extremely sugary coffee. I think she put five creamers and double that in sugar packets in that little cup.

"You're staring," she says, turning her attention back to me.

"I'm thinking," I murmur, smiling behind my own cup of coffee.

"That's scary."

"I'm thinking I'd like to get to know you more," I confess, leaning forward to gauge her reaction.

"I think we know each other pretty well," she laughs as Wanda sits our food down in front of us. When she walks away, Holly continues. "You probably know me better than any other person I've been with."

"You know what I mean," I tell her, my eyes narrowing on her playfully as she takes an impressive bite of the pancakes. "I want to learn things about you outside of the bedroom. I mean, I'd love to continue to explore everything about that tight little body of yours inside the bedroom. But I'd also like to know your favorite food and if you organize your books by title or genre. You know, the big stuff."

"Mmm," she hums, smiling and nodding her head. "The big stuff."

"I'll even buy all the sugar and creamer the store has in stock to make sure you have enough to make your coffee exactly as you like it when you stay over."

"Ha ha ha." She gives me a look of fake annoyance and fights a smile. "You do realize I just got out of a relationship that lasted half a decade, right?"

"I do," I say. "And we can go as slow as you want. I'm not in any sort of rush. I'm just not ready for this to be over. I've been around long enough to know that when something feels right, you go for it. And you feel right."

"That's what she said."

She laughs, and I roll my eyes at how cute she is when she's feeling awkward.

"Okay," she says. "Yeah, I'm not done with this either."

I feel the smile take over my entire face at her words. I know I need to tread carefully, not letting myself get too eager and scare her away. This needs to go at her pace if it's going to work.

She leans forward and puts her elbow on the table, extending her pinky finger in my direction.

"We go slow, yeah?"

"We go slow," I agree, linking my pinky with hers.

"Now we kiss it," she says, leaning over the table to place her lips on the promise. "To seal the deal."

"I'd rather kiss you," I tell her but kiss my thumb to seal the pinky promise anyway. Before she can slip back into her seat, I reach over and grab the back of her head, pulling her in for a quick kiss.

She tastes like coffee and cinnamon, and when we both sink back into our seats, her face is redder than I've ever seen it. That makes me wonder if that tiny amount of public affection can make her blush that hard, what would happen if I introduced a toy?

That was definitely going on my list of things to try with her.

As I watch her continue to eat her breakfast, every once in a while looking out of the window to watch the snow, I realize how excited I am to get to know this woman. She seems so different from the person I saw with tearstained cheeks and red-rimmed eyes last night.

There's a weight that's been lifted, and I can tell despite the circumstances, she's happy to be out of that situation. A huge gust of wind blows the snow down even harder, covering the cars outside in a thick layer of the stuff. She looks back over to me, smiling and finishing off her sugar water.

"What're you doing for New Year's?" I ask her.

"Spending it with you?" she asks, her face turning mischievous as she looks over at me.

"Good girl."

To be continued...?

ACKNOWLEDGMENTS

This was just for fun, and I hope you all enjoyed it. This was to test the waters and see how everyone would react to a very light Daddy kink. I'd like to go full on in a later book so...

Huge thanks to Cassie at Opulent Designs for fitting me in at the last minute and making a cover I absolutely adore.

Thanks to all my friends for beta reading it and encouraging me throughout. I'm so glad you all loved Daddy Nick just as much as I did.

Sandra, thank you for putting up with my chaos for the last few months...it's been a wild ride, girl. Finger's crossed 2022 will run a bit smoother?

OTHER WORKS

The Triad Series
Scars: https://www.amazon.com/dp/B092R48WNW
Liars: https://www.amazon.com/dp/B094R92GLX
Omens: https://www.amazon.com/dp/B09KTCVG9F

The One Night Series
Games We Play: https://www.amazon.com/dp/B094MZT5RC
Secrets We Hunt: https://www.amazon.com/dp/B0994Y4PWC
Burdens We Carry: https://www.amazon.com/dp/B09M8NW8CJ

Standalone
Into The Dark: https://www.amazon.com/dp/B097QKB339
Into The Dark (White Cover): https://www.amazon.com/dp/B09KN7WQ3D

ABOUT THE AUTHOR

Dana Isaly is a writer of dark romance, fantasy romance, and has also been known to dabble in poetry (it was a phase in college, leave her alone).

She was born in the midwest and has been all over but now resides (begrudgingly) in Alabama. She is a lover of books, coffee, and rainy days. Dana is probably the only person in the writing community that is actually a morning person.

She swears too much, is way too comfortable on her TikTok (@authordanaisaly and @auth.danaisaly), and believes that love is love is love.

You can find her on Instagram (@danaisalyauthorpage) or on Facebook with the same name, but she won't lie, Facebook is not her forte.

Made in United States
Orlando, FL
07 January 2022